Jean-Luc Fromental / Joëlle Jolivet

D1292732

365
PENGUINS

Abrams Books for Young Readers
New York

On New Year's Day, at nine o'clock in the morning,
a delivery man rang our doorbell.

I opened the box—**a penguin!**
Who sent us such a strange gift?

We looked for the sender's name all around the box.
Nothing.

"Look," said my sister, Amy.

"Strange," said my father.

I'm number 1, feed me when I'm hungry.

The next morning:

Ding dong!

Penguin number 2.

On the box, there was still no name, no address. **Nothing.**

Only a note, slightly different this time:

I'm number 2 and, like number 1, I need you to take care of me.

And it went on like that until the end of the week.

On Sunday, we had **7** penguins in our house.

On Monday morning, during breakfast,
we had a big discussion about naming the penguins.

"No need to argue," Mommy
said. "I don't think . . ."

". . . we're going to keep them!"

At the end of January, there were thirty-one penguins in the house.

No more, no less.

February has only twenty-eight days. Each morning another penguin arrived. That made:

$$31 + 28 = ??$$

59 penguins!

And number 60 on the next day.

But there was a problem . . .

What should we do with all these penguins?

"Give them away," Mommy suggested.

Daddy had a better idea:
"We should organize them!"

"Four times fifteen equals sixty!" Daddy said.
"You only have to know how to count . . ."

Ding dong!

"Plus one!"

On April the tenth exactly, penguin number **100** arrived.

"This weird sense of humor reminds me of someone," Mommy said.

After the first three-digit number, our problems really began.

HERE WERE

SOME OF THEM:

2) Taking care of the penguins

We didn't have to clean them, but . . .

Me first! **I'm late!**

Their favorite room was the bathroom. They made bathing in the morning a bit difficult for our family.

Aargh! I hate penguins!

Penguins, penguins everywhere,
Black and white and in my hair.
Two or three would be quite nice,
But hundreds more, let's think twice!
Bathroom, bedroom, closet, kitchen—
I've had enough, it's time to ditch 'em!

Amy is right. It's time to make a serious decision.

3) Housing the penguins

Desperate times call for desperate measures! Ted—get the hammer and the saw!

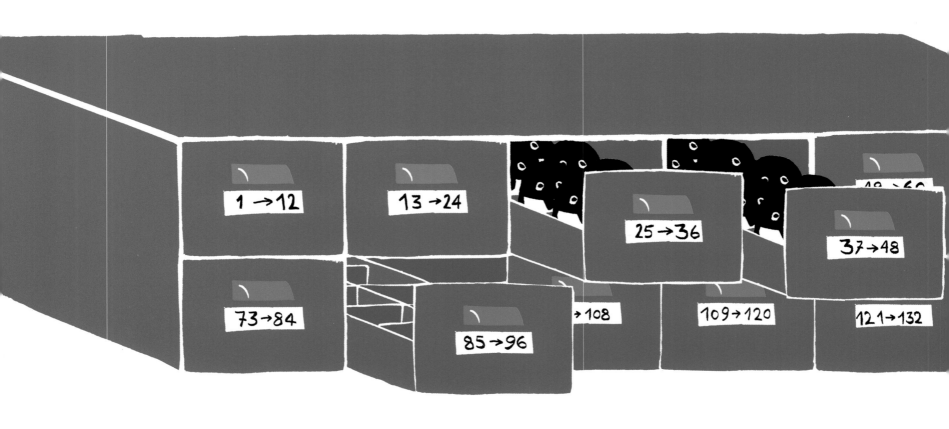

The days went by and penguins piled up.

On May twenty-fourth, we had 144 penguins.

When summer arrived, there were new complications:

a) The heat

Penguins are not used to warm climates. When the temperature rises, they become restless.

b) The noise
180 restless penguins sound like a playground at recess.

c) Let's not talk about the other problems . . .

On the fourth of August, a gleam of hope: Daddy found a new way of storing the penguins!

A cube = 6 x 6 x 6 = ???

Unfortunately, this was a short-term solution . . .

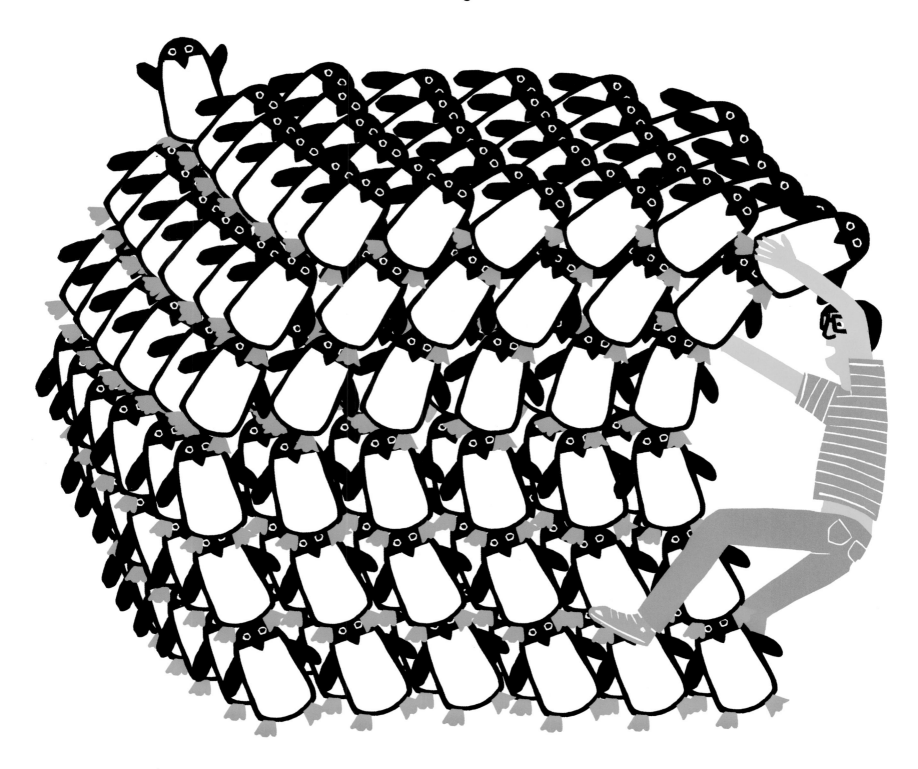

Here's another note!

This silly sense of humor reminds me of someone . . .

217 is here . . . and the end isn't near!

Once you've reached the point of no return, one penguin more or one penguin less each day doesn't make much difference anymore.

You live penguin.

You think penguin.

You dream penguin.

You become penguin.

Before we could say **"kwak,"**
it was the end of the year.

On December thirty-first, 365 guests
in dinner jackets were in the house.
But we had New Year's Eve on the lawn.

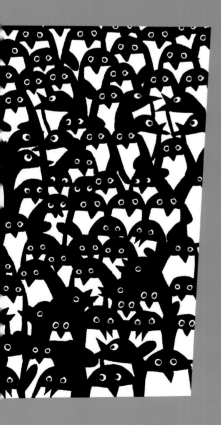

Ding
dong!

364 . . . 365 . . .
You're all here, my dears.
Even you, my little Chilly,
with your blue feet!

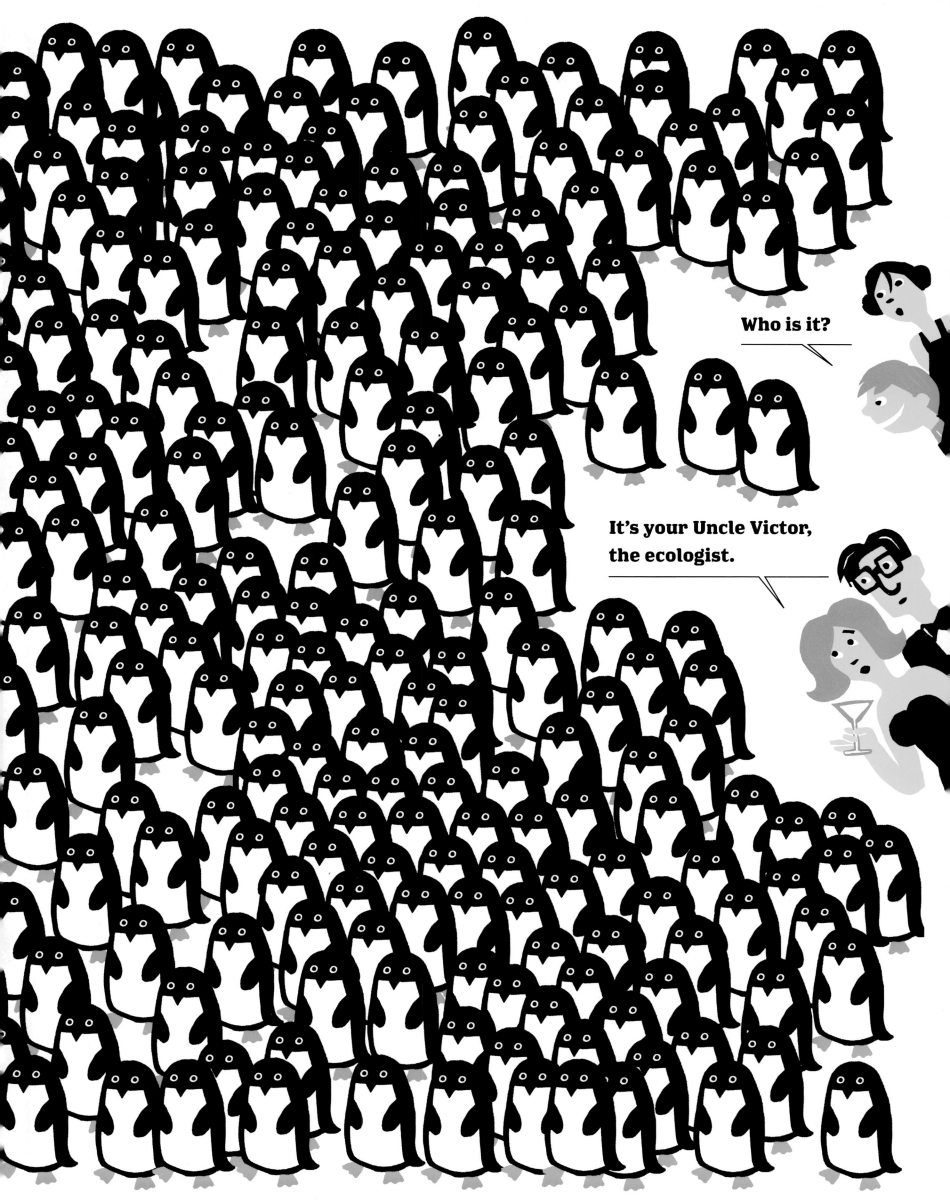

Then Uncle Victor explained to us:

As you know, the planet is heating up. The ice caps are melting. Year after year, these lovely birds of the South Pole see their territory get smaller and smaller. To increase their chances of survival, I decided to introduce them to the North Pole. But, unfortunately, you can't export endangered species. So I found an expensive but secret way: sending one penguin a day to your family during one year—one day a male, the other day a female. 182 couples equals 364 penguins, plus this little Chilly, who's so cute with his little blue feet. That's 365 penguins. Your old Uncle Victor is not so crazy!

But he still has a terrible sense of humor!

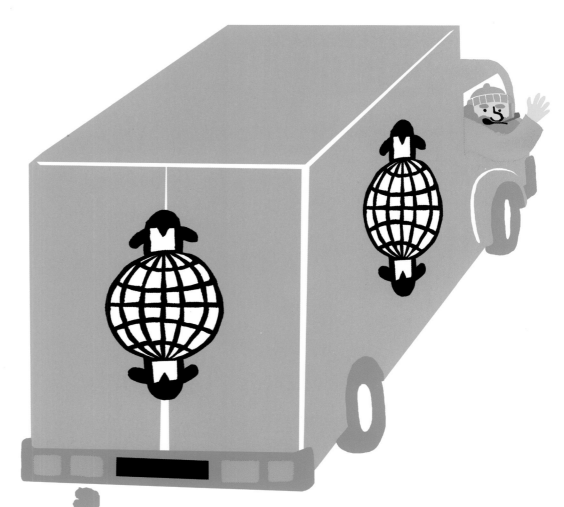

Then Uncle Victor left with all his penguins—except one.

We'll take care of you, Chilly.

And life started to return to normal . . .

But the next day,

the delivery man came to the door.

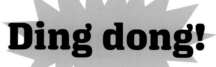

Ding dong!